Library of Congress Cataloging in Publication Data:
Elliott, Dan. Grover learns to read. (A Sesame Street start-to-read book) SUMMARY: Because he wants his mother to continue reading to him at bedtime, Grover is reluctant to tell her that he knows how to read. 1. Children's stories, American. [1. Reading—Fiction. 2. Puppets—Fiction] I. Chartier, Normand, 1945–   ill. II. Title. III. Series: Sesame Street start-to-read books. PZ7.E446Gt   1985   [E]   84-27692
ISBN: 0-394-87498-6 (trade); 0-394-97498-0 (lib. bdg.)

Manufactured in the United States of America   0

Grover Learns to Read

by Dan Elliott
illustrated by Normand Chartier

Featuring Jim Henson's Sesame Street Muppets

Random House / Children's Television Workshop

Grover was happy.

He was in his cozy bed.

And his mother was reading
a bedtime story to him.

"And they lived happily
ever after. The end,"
read Grover's mother.
Then she tucked Grover in.

"Soon you will be reading books
all by yourself," she said.
"Just think! My little Grover—
in school and learning to read!"
She kissed him good night
and said, "Sleep tight."

But Grover did not sleep tight.
He tossed and turned.
"Read books all by myself?"
he said to his pillow.
"I want my mommy
to read to me!"

The next day in school
Grover's teacher wrote some words
on the blackboard.

"Who can read this?"
asked the teacher.
"ME!" Grover said.
And he read the words out loud.
"Very good!" the teacher said.

Grover sang all the way home.
"I, Grover, am so smart.
Mommy will be so proud.
I, Grover, can read out loud!"

Suddenly he stopped singing.
"But I do not want
to read out loud.
I want Mommy to read to ME
and tuck me in
and kiss me good night.
From now on I will try
NOT to learn to read."

When Grover got home,
his mother gave him
some milk and cookies.
"How was school?" she asked.
"Did you have a reading lesson?"
Grover said, "Yes."
"Good!" said his mother.
"And what did you learn?"
Grover thought about it.
"Nothing," he said.
"Oh, my! Nothing at all?"
asked his mother.
Grover did not answer.

That night Grover's mother
read his favorite story—
"Goldilocks and the Three Bears."
Grover was able to read
some of the words himself.
Oh, how he wanted to tell her!
But he said nothing.

And every day after school,
when his mother asked,
"What did you learn
in school today?"
Grover said, "Nothing."

Then he would say,
"Read me a story, Mommy."
His mother would smile
and say, "In a minute."
And she always did read him
a story, but sometimes
it was a very long minute.

One day after school
Grover was playing in the park.
Betty Lou came running up.
"Grover, do me a favor," she said.
"I have to take these books
back to the library.
Will you watch my baby sister?
I'll be back in a minute."

"Yes, I, Grover the baby sitter,
will be so happy to watch
your baby sister," he said.

Betty Lou left—
and the baby started to cry.
Grover tried to make
the baby stop crying.
He stood on his head.

He made funny faces.
But the baby just screamed
louder and louder.

"Oh, dear, where is Betty Lou?
This is a VERY long minute!"
he said.
The baby picked up Grover's book
and put it in her mouth.

"No!" said Grover.
"Books are not for eating.
Books are for reading!
I, Grover, will show you."
He opened the book
and began to read.

"Once upon a time..."
read Grover.
The baby stopped crying.
She crawled onto Grover's lap
and smiled.

Soon Betty Lou came back.

"Thanks a lot, Grover," she said.

"Oh, it was nothing,"

he said happily.

Grover ran home
to tell his mother.
"Mommy, I read a story
to Betty Lou's baby sister!
She sat in my lap
just like I sit in yours!"

His mother smiled.
"Grover, I did not know
you learned how to read!"
And she gave him a big hug.
"Yes, I am a super reader,"
he said.

"That is wonderful!"
said Grover's mother.
"No, it is not," he said sadly.
"Now you will stop reading to me."
Grover's mother looked surprised.
"Why, I love reading to you!
And I always will.
But now you can read
to me too sometimes!"

"Oh, Mommy!" Grover said happily.
"That's a great idea!"
And he opened a book
and read a story to her
right then.

That night, after Grover's mother
read him a story
and tucked him in, she said,
"Let's go to the library tomorrow.
It is time for you to get
a library card."
Then she kissed him good night
and said, "Sleep tight."
And that is just what he did.

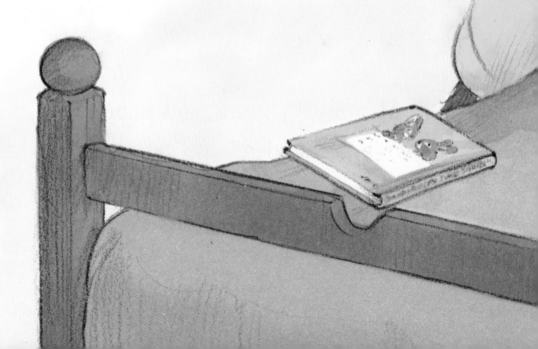

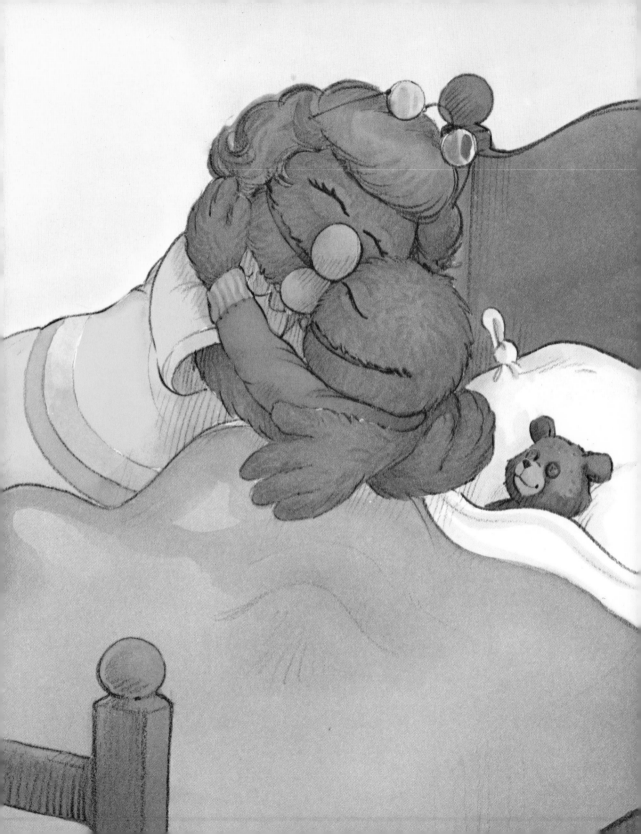

The next day Grover got
his very own library card.
He borrowed six wonderful books.
The librarian waved good-bye.
"Enjoy your books!" she said.
And Grover did!